What Is It?

a modern look at love

What Is It?

a modern look at love

David Alan Royster

Formatting: Enchanted Ink Publishing

ISBN: 9780578196206

Printed in the United States of America

This book is dedicated to Denes, Camila, and Armand. Because of you, I do my best not to be careless with this life. Also, to my grandpa Clyde, a man famous for few words and plenty of action. I carry you all in my **heart,** daily.

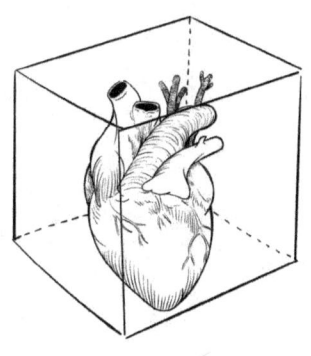

CONTENTS

CONNECT WITH DAVID ALAN ROYSTER

Social Media - @davidalanroyster

PREFACE

I didn't want to write a book about it. It started when my ex-girlfriend broke up with me. I've always had a passion for writing, even while I was with her, but the dedication to a daily dose of composition came after we went our separate ways. I started writing exactly how I felt, describing every ache in detail. I only posted it to Instagram because I was copying my best friend, and I thought some accountability couldn't hurt. I didn't expect people to respond how they did.

I started getting messages from IG'ers saying I was writing exactly how they felt. Someone even said, "I've seen good writers, but what you do with words is magic." These types of compliments can make a man feel good, really good. I started posting every day, and then people began demanding a book. I told them I'd put one together. It was more of a joke than an actual response, but they didn't think it was as funny as I did. In an effort to be a man of my word, I did a thing. So, here it is. A book.

Where It Starts

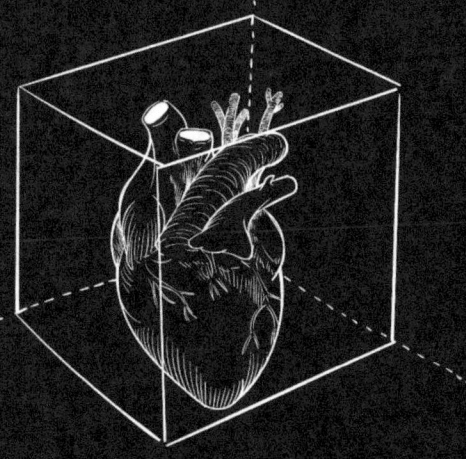

I was a poem
She was a melody
Songs emerged
Between us.

    – COMPOSITION

Why do I feel
Like the stars
Gaze at you.

GAZE –

Love is tugging
At strings
That could very well
Pull me apart.

— (INSPIRED BY @PARRY_ELWAHEY) —

"Hell" is being a lover
With no one to love

The fires you burn in
Are your own.

– DESIRE –

We were young
And unknowing

But her love
Was as ripe

As the sweet pink apples
From my grandmother's orchard.

– PINK APPLES

There's a difference

Between needing me,

And needing me

For now.

DIFFERENT NEEDS –

As fast as my heart is beating
Can we just take it slow?
These texts are flying faster
Than my common sense can go

I slipped and said I love you
How can I really know?
The real you doesn't know me;
It's just starting to show

And contact with my skin
Is not contact with my soul
And this contact high we have,
Does it connect us in the lows?

I don't know what is waiting
When the drama's out of the curtain,
Can it hold? Or will it fold?
Is anybody ever certain?

Am I getting way ahead?
Am I jumping the gun?
Are we supposed to see what happens?
Do we do whatever's fun?

I'm just being cautious
Cause breakups come with pain
I just want to give you all of me
And not give you me in vain

So can we not rush through?
Can we not skip pages?
Can we do love like wine?
Can we sip it through the ages?

Can we really get to see
Where we're going before we go?
It's not that I DON'T love you,
I just really want to know...

– CAN I LOVE YOU SLOW? –

"Keep going that way. Something will get in your way. And if it's good—or if it's something worth holding onto, you're gonna pick it up and put it in your pocket.

Everything else is trash."

I've always wanted a woman
Who loves like a soldier
And fights like a poet

Always with unfailing
Faithfulness

Always for the yearning
In her heart.

WOMAN –

Even though
It's taboo
To say it this early

I think we'd have
A happy life
Together.

– SAY IT EARLY TO THE WOMAN AT THE DRIVE-THRU WINDOW –

We drew our hearts in the sand
For the tide to wash it out,
It wasn't anyone's fault but ours
For pressing our way unnaturally.

– THE TIDE –

Forgive me, if in return for a kiss
I ask you, "Did you eat?"

I was never taught
To say "love"

Just be it.

   – MUTE

I put a note
In her pocket—
A parting gift

"Find the one
Who makes you smile"

I could tell by her face
She'd look for me
In every man
From here on out.

IRONY –

Ultimately,
It was her taste of music
That drew me into her song.

– HER MUSIC –

I want you all the time,
Especially when I'm with you.

– WANT –

If meeting you
Was "falling" in
Love

That explains why
Leaving you
Was flight.

     – OPPOSITES

All this time
Love was said
To be hard

You have
Reminded me
How gentle, too
It can be

LOVE IS EASY 1 –

Everything in life
I've worked hard for
What makes you think
I'd do you different?

– ROUTINE –

I was chewin on some fried chicken momma bought earlier. And then I saw you walk in. You was my brother's friend. You came in lookin like a wet peach. I had to put my wing down. I had to get healthy. You turned me to a vegantarian instantly. All I wanted was a bite.

– HEALTHY –

It was strange when she found out I'm just a man. I don't know why she was surprised. I had been telling her all along. But she insisted I was Prince Charming or whatever. Funny. I used thousands of words but couldn't paint a new picture in her mind. She told her friends I might as well have slipped a glass flat on her foot.

And then one day she woke up. She saw me. Not the projection of me in her mind. But me. And she didn't like it. And she left me. I don't know who's to blame for the way my heart is aching. I told her the truth. I gave her honesty. There's no reward for that?

She was like jazz music

Just when you thought
You had her rhythm

She'd change up and take you
To a different pace.

JAZZMYN –

Promise
You'll always be this way

Time after time and
day after day

When eyes go blind
and hair is gray

Promise
You'll always be this way.

– PROMISE –

I need to get back
To real relationships—
Women that can
Bring me Heaven

But in the meantime

I want the bad broads
To give me Hell.

– TIME TO ADMIT IT –

Things to do before I die:
Tell her how I feel inside.

– To Do List

Provided that
He only broke
You into pieces

You still have it all,
Like a pizza in slices
Every. bite. delicious.

You may not feel whole,
But you are no less
Because of a feeling.

No Less –

I spent weeks
Chasing a woman
Who did not want
My love

I wrote her letters
And bought her gifts,
Took her to parties,
Made her mother laugh

And, still,
She did not give me
What I asked for

I forgot my mother's advice
All those years ago:
Stop dancing!
This is not your song.

– **WRONG SONG** –

"You don't have to be looking. If it's something worth finding, it'll stand out."

❤

She plays my note,

Though out of tune

It's her favorite key
To touch

And I squeal
An awful cadence
That makes her
Crescendoing smile
Pull me a few pitches
Higher.

OUT OF TUNE –

I'm done
Getting drunk
On people
Who leave me
Sitting
On the curb.

– BREAK OFF THE HENNY –

We knew love
Because
We didn't know
Any better.

– BLISS –

"The only time I dance is with her.
She doesn't mind that I suck."

Let's be invisible
To everyone but us

And dance

In our own little corner
Of the world.

OUR OWN –

There it goes again
That dumb feeling
All fingers and no tongue
When I think of you.

– SPEECHLESS –

Love is dead—
No brains
No hearts

Just zombies
Groping each other.

– ZOMBIES –

You stare at red
And hope it's blue

All metaphors aside—

If he loved you
He would love you

All metaphors aside.

    – METAPHORS

Most of our love
Gets caught in our throats
And never quite reaches
Where it wants to go.

INTENTIONS –

How full
I've become
Since you've
Come around.

– FULL –

You have curves
In all the right places

But if my heart chose you,
It's you

Which means I love
All your curves
And all your edges too.

– CURVES –

"She'll come when you least expect it. Like, Dawg. You're not even gonna be thinking about it. It's just gonna happen, and you're gonna be like, 'what the heck.'"

Then the right one
Came along
Like spring
After the rain
Turning disaster
Into desire,
Making purpose
Out of pain.

THE RIGHT ONE –

No one wants you
Until someone wants you,
Then everyone wants you
Until no one wants you

It begs the question:
Do you want you?
Or are you just waiting
For someone?

– EPIDEMIC –

When my soul is broken
And the green fire flares,
I need more than thicc thighs
To push me through

I need a woman
With aiding arms and
The mind of Aristotle.

– THICC –

Talk until the lights die down
And the chill calls for covers
Talk until the movie has ended
And only crumbs are in the bowl
Talk until your tea is cold
And the dogs retire from barking
Talk until you forget
What you were talking about
Talk until my eyelids lock their gates
And my breath whispers gentle songs
Talk until the sun lifts its head
And the sprinklers cackle over the grass
Talk until your soul is full
And your heart is laid empty

Talk to me.

     – TALK

Where It Goes

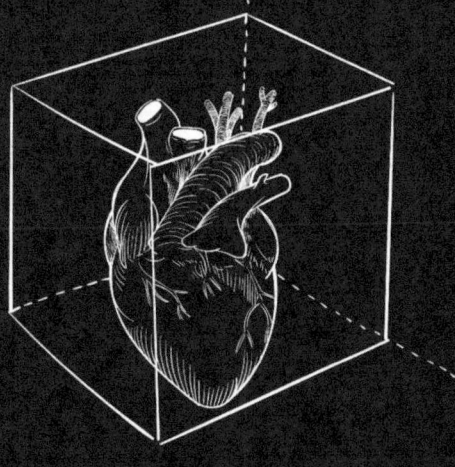

"Everyone can look good for two seconds.
Everyone can play the role. It takes time
to see who they are."

♥

Sometimes it's not your spirit
I want to be touched by.

Sinner's Prayer –

I could watch you all day
And never change the channel.

– HBU –

She's not better than you;
She's more consistent
But that makes her better
For me.

— NONCOMPARATIVE COMPARISONS —

I prayed for you

Before I knew your name
And the color of your fingertips,
I knelt down on hardwood floors
And asked God
For someone who could bend light—
Clear darkness clean
From my memory, so that I
Don't know when to sleep,
But also for someone
Who could give me rest

I rest my head on your chest
I rest my head on your lap,
Rest my head on the promises
You know how to keep

I submitted myself
Before God
To find Heaven on Earth,
But I guess an angel
Was all that He had left

And even after,
Now that you're mine
I still pray for you.

ANSWERED –

Love is loyalty.

– JUST SAYIN' –

Sleep in faith,
My heart is yours
Even when
You close your eyes.

– TRUST –

It's okay to get upset

Pound on my chest,
If you need to

Get it out,
But don't get out

Don't walk away
From "us"

Don't hurt me in ways
That don't heal.

    – DON'T

Do we have to
Sophisticate our feelings
As we get older?

Can it not be you're pretty
With a dope soul,
And I want to be with you
For as long as we've got?

UNSOPHISTICATE IT –

I'm only ever in two places-
                        With you,

            Or on the way.

        – HOME SOON –

I can't promise
To love you every day
Like other men have

But I can promise
To be here every day
Like they haven't.

– PROMISES –

"I could not stand her"
Turned into
"I could not stand to be
Without her."

– 15 WORDS, A LOVE STORY

Like I'm not allowed
To love both
your body and mind

When the truth is
I want to dive
into both.

DUALITY –

For once
I would like to feel
Like there's someone
Missing out on me.

– F.O.M.O –

She was a poem
That didn't wait
To be written
Or need
To be read

She existed on
Her own page
Whether you were on it
Or not

That is why
I chose her.

– POEM –

I've long since stopped
Measuring love by
Text messages per day

Cause when that chemistry
Gets finicky,
Those numbers will change.

    – SURE SIGNS

You are the song
Sung by flowers

And the dance
Danced by trees

You are the bird
You are the bees

You are the bee's knees.

NECTAR –

My fingers stroll
Down your spine
One vertebra
At a time

Like children
Crossing a river
With nowhere
To go in mind.

– VERTEBRA –

Algorithms
Brought us
Together

It's in our destiny
To beat the odds.

– COMPUTER LOVE –

What if love
Is not blind

But the only time
We see clearly.

– LOVE IS BLIND

I've been dismantling women
Since the time I was torn
From my mother's womb

I ground you to dust
And blew you to the wind
To see how many directions
I could scatter you in

And like the dust you are
Still everywhere.

DISMANTLE –

You do not have to try so hard
To hurt me. It comes naturally.

– ORGANIC –

You will lose
What you don't
Hold onto.

– OBVIOUSLY –

The heart
Is the biggest jester
Of all

Making fools of
The wisest men
And loneliest women.

    – JESTER

I wear your love
Like a sweater
On the coldest days
Of winter.

WORN –

To have you
Is to burn in flames

To give you up
Is to live in the dark.

– DARK –

Your number
Is still saved,
Just in case
I'm wrong.

– HUMAN ERROR –

I just want to go back
To when your eyes were a haven
Instead of a place of shame
And your shoulder was a warmer bed
Than the couch

I just want to go back
To when your questions were inquisitive
Rather than rhetorical
And your mouth was something
I wanted to hear

I just want to go back
To when sleepless nights
Were adventures to smile through
Instead of the torment
They are today

I just want to go back
To when all we needed
Was a pinky promise
To ensure that my words were true

I just want to go back
To me and you.

THE CHALLENGE –

You must write
Your promises
In pencil

The way you
Erase
So casually
Your mistakes.

– In Pencil –

Sometimes my hands
They feel like my heart

Want to touch you somewhere
But don't know where to start.

– HEART HANDS –

"Don't log on my Netflix anymore.
Once again, using me how you do."

I still sleep with the light on
And the cover folded back
Holding onto any chance
You might be coming to bed.

COME TO BED –

I have kissed her in places
Other men have not seen
And don't even know how
To get to.

– HUBRIS –

Your mouth does things
Your hands could never
Like tear me to pieces
And hold me together.

– WHAT THAT MOUTH DO? –

You don't have to
Convince me
To love you,
There's something in you
That I want
To love.

     – PROVE

Am I the only one
Not chasing a soulmate,
Allowing my life to activate
Allowing my soul to acclimate.

JOURNEY ALONE –

You give me more than enough
Reasons to kiss you

But I don't need one,
And never did.

– It's Just You –

Isn't it time
I stop comparing
Your eyes to the stars
And your body
To the river's bend

As if those
Age-old wonders
Could contain you.

– CONTAINERS –

I'm sure we'll reach forever,
If we make it through tonight.

– ONE DAY AT A TIME

Her machine gun tongue
And my bulletproof pride
Make for one hell of a war.

WAR –

Despite everything I've heard
About love being hard to manage,
You make it feel like falling asleep—
I let my guard down and dream.

– LOVE IS EASY 2 –

I cannot do it

I can't be your man,

You love with your mouth

But not with your hand.

– My Love Language is Touch –

"It's hard. Ya'll single people swear you want the real deal, but some people make dumb moves. Dumb moves."

Girls fall for
The dumbest stuff

How'd she let her brother
Pin her in a wrestling game
And leave sores on her neck

Dumb.

DUMB –

When I find it,
I will sing to it
Every song I can remember
And hum the parts I don't

When I find it,
I'll walk beside it
On the side of oncoming cars
To protect it from harm

When I find it,
I'll stare into it
With hanging jaw
And loose lip,
Bewildered and in awe
Of its beauty

When I find it,
I'll hold it in my arms,
Pressed against
My pounding heart
Because it makes me
Feel alive

When I find it,
I won't have to go too far,
It will be outside my window,
Looking in

It will be laughing
Beside my winded body,
It will be praying
For direction in my life,
It will tell me
When I stink

When I find it,
It will be
The greatest treasure
Ever found

And when I'm older
And my children
gather around,
I will tell them
I didn't find it

Instead,
I was found.

– When I Find It –

Put your heart
In my hands

No more questions.

– REST ASSURED

Like the moon
Reflecting the sun,
I shine brighter
Around you.

AROUND YOU –

I can feel
The distance

Silence,
Like a ton of bricks,
Pushes down on my shoulders
As I wait
For an "I love you"
That isn't coming

Like glass,
I can see the cracks
In your eyes,
Where the truth
Is flooding out
And filling the room

You'll break
If I do this
But I want to hold
Your hand

– GLASS –

"Relationships don't run on autopilot.
You have to keep course correcting."

I'm looking
For who will love

After the love
Is gone.

AND AFTER? –

there are millions
of twinkling stars
illuminating
the dark

but my world
revolves around
just one.

– JUST ONE –

I've backed myself
Into a corner
To make room for you.

– THE SHRINKING MAN –

"Any relationship is going to take work.
It's going to be stress and work, especially if you want a good one."

The opposite
Of love
Is a lack
Of effort.

EFFORT –

There isn't a story
Worth telling
That doesn't hurt
At least a little

There isn't a love
Worth having
That never gets
Cold or brittle

Continue.

– CONTINUE –

I won't pretend
That I admire your thorns
Or say
They don't hurt me

But I'll still hold you
While my hand bleeds
Cause pain is the price
Of love.

– WHILE MY HAND BLEEDS –

My superwoman cries
And bleeds
And occasionally needs
Some ice cream

That makes her
No less
The woman who best
Carries the weight
Of my world.

    – **SUPERWOMAN**

How freeing it is
To take the blame
For the condition of
My own heart

It's almost as if
I own it.

PINK SLIP –

I'd tell you
How beautiful
You look today

But there's not
Enough time
Before sunset

To tell how
You set fire
To a sundress

My mouth
Is overflowing
From yesterday.

– RUNNING BEHIND –

I dare not break
The silence
That binds us;
It's all we have left
To hold onto.

— SOMETHING —

Buttered popcorn, instant lover
Tears in my heart recovered

A billion bad years
Painted over by summer

A million blue days
Painted over in yellow

Crushing goodbyes lifted
By a single hello

The pain left so fast you would think someone stole it
The bad taste washed out by a microwave moment

Memories of misery are instantly out of mind
Pushed aside by a teaspoon of time

With the one who's present.

  – INSTANT LOVER

What extraordinary things I'd do
To have another ordinary argument
With you.

TAKE ME BACK –

Like fries tucked
In the crease of my
Car seat

Girl, we're here
Forever.

– LOVE GREASE –

Where It Ends

Are You Ready?

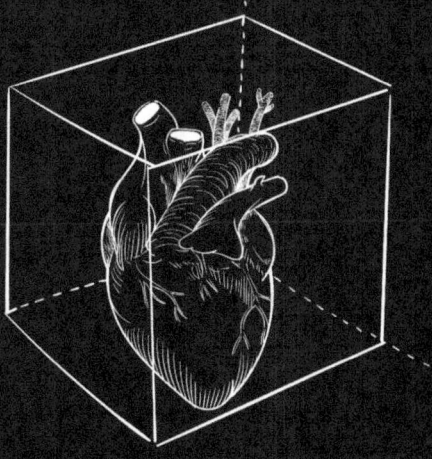

Your kisses do
To my skin
What the morning
Does to daisies.

    – DAISIES

It took me a long time
To get away from you

Even after I left

It took me a long time
To view independence
As a celebration.

INDEPENDENCE DAY –

It's not love
If I only call
At eleven PM.

– Eleven –

Women should serve men

Men should serve women

Any house of peace
Is full of servants.

– HIERARCHY OF A HOME –

You could be anywhere in the world,
Yet you're right here
In my corner.

— IN MY CORNER

I built a life
Around the words
You easily deserted

What else could I do
But come to ruin.

RUIN –

We crumbled under
The tremendous weight
Of little things.

– LITTLE THINGS –

Loving with our paper hearts—
We don't even remember
The shape we took
Or the bends we made
To get here.

– PAPER HEARTS –

"Many of you are taking anything
because you don't know what you want."

There is no value
That can be placed
On a woman
Who turns everything
She touches
Into gold.

QUEEN MIDAS –

I don't trust my heart

Most of my pain
Is because of it.

– TRUST ISSUES –

She does not
Have to do
Everything

To be everything
To me

But what she does do
Is everything
Anyway.

– TO ME –

It's funny how
I'd be lying
If I didn't say
I miss you

But other times
My silence tells
All the truth
In the world.

       – QUIET LIE

Years go by like seconds
When you're with the one you love,
So I have a small question
About forever...

SMALL TALK –

It's amazing what passes
For love these days—
Crows parading as blue jays.

– BLUE JAYS –

I love you
With all of my heart

And then some.

– MORE THAN MY HEART –

Love begins
At the end of pride

– LOVE BEGINS

These days,
People break up
Out of boredom—
My mother would
Kill me!

UPBRINGING –

We've spent too long
Pulling in all directions
When surrender was the way
To find the light.

— SURRENDER —

Just because
I'm only
A stone throw
Away

Does not give
You permission
To keep throwing
Stones

Stop.

– STONE'S THROW –

One day I'll learn
How to show my heart
To people
Without putting it
In their hands.

    – LOOK, BUT DON'T TOUCH

You can have the last laugh

There's no more humor in the way
We destroy our better halves.

WHITE FLAG –

He turns you off and on
With his childlike hands,
Will you ever burn out
Will you ever cease giving
All of your energy
To his abuse.

– LIGHTBULB –

I thought we could clear the air
If we said what's on our minds

But we were chasing peace
By launching all our missiles
At once

Maybe when,
When the dust settles,
We'll learn
to hold our tongues
And each other.

– ON OUR MINDS –

"Nobody said wife her. Bruh. Smash that. She's ready, bro. You know, and when she tries to get all clingy, let her know. 'Ay, that's not what it is.'"

❤

Destinee
Adrienne
Dulce
Hannah
Kristen

And the list goes on.
I have done the worst
To way too many girls
To still think
That I'm a good guy

And yet I can't
Tell my side of the story
Without my friends saying,
"They didn't deserve you."

GOOD GUY –

Sometimes
We do wrong
Just because
We can.

– CAPABLE –

All it takes
Is a tiny spark
To start a large and
Uncontrollable fire

All it took was
One word spoken
Too fast.

— SPARK —

"Here comes the good part,"
Is what God said
When he introduced you
In my story.

– THE GOOD PART

We weren't meant to be,
But accidents have made
Indispensable things.

INDISPENSABLE —

I'm a student of your heart

Studying the ways
To make you feel
My love.

– STUDY TIME –

Dear Beloved,

Don't worry

The right one
Is still looking
Too.

Sincerely,

Destiny

– DESTINY'S LETTER –

It's terrifying—

What I've done to you
In the name of love.

– IN WHAT POWER

All these partners
And no one is
Working together

All these lovers
And no one
Is giving love.

MISNAMED –

Maybe these scars
Are not scars at all

Maybe God was
Sewing patience
Beneath my skin

So I wouldn't be so quick
To jump out of it.

– TRIBULATION WORKETH PATIENCE –

Men have tendency to forget
That wisdom is a woman.

– PROVERB –

The aches in my forearms
From loving her

The cracking of my spine
From loving her

The lightning in my chest
From loving her

The fire behind my ears
From loving her—

The anger and pain
From loving her

She rolled over in the morning. I could tell she had been up for a while. "Do you still love me?" she asked.

I responded the only way my pride would allow, "Why do you ask dumb questions?"

– DUMB QUESTIONS

My tired eyes fight
To look at you
A little longer.

5 More Minutes –

My mother didn't raise me to give up;
I will always be the one left behind.

– TRAGEDY –

I've never seen such
A riveting performance
Of love

That whole time
I never knew
You were acting.

– THE SHOW –

"Sometimes you have to let your wife loose on people. Other times you have to say, 'Baby, chill out.'"

♥

My heart was as hard as a rock,
But your hands were like water

Little by little

Softening me.

SOFT –

You slip on a cape
When you tell your friends
What came between us

I'm not the bad guy,
But I'll play the enemy
If that's what you need
To save yourself.

– VILLAINS AND HEROES –

I have a lot of thoughts
That should never have made it
To words.

– To Words –

When they told me to f*ck
As many women as I can,
They didn't tell me I'd leave
Each one a piece of me

They didn't tell me I'd leave
Empty handed, and hearted.

– **WHAT THEY DON'T SAY**

I know it's hard to believe
I want you to be happy
You'll see it too

When you stop calling.

HAPPY FOR YOU –

I just remembered
My first love

It was not you

It was me.

– My First Love –

My biggest mistake
Was looking for God
In you.

– SAVIOR –

Put your words away
And talk to me.

   – Bullets

Everything I've ever done
Was because I love you

Including when I
Said, "Goodbye."

IT'S BECAUSE –

The only thing worse
Than loving you
Is not.

– A ROCK AND A HEART PLACE –

Give attention
To the ones
Who gaze at you
Like a lunatic—

The madly
In pursuit

The ones who row
Through storms
In a paddle boat
And risk sinking
To carry you
Above the waves

Those are the ones.
Trust me.

– MY ADVICE –

"It may not be pretty on paper, but it's hard. I also think it's more romantic, you know? It's more romantic to put in hard work than you're smitten all the time. I don't know."

I want to be
Bored with you
And take the time
To reignite fires
That we once had

Picking out
My favorite parts of you
All over again

Retracing my steps
Through your mind
To make sure I didn't miss
The smallest detail

Making sure I
Know these roads
Like my childhood
Neighborhood

I want to know you
And know you
And know you.

MONOTONOUS –

I'm so scared
Of spending my time
With the wrong woman;
Kings come to ruin that way.

– WHY ARE YOU SINGLE? –

I'd lick the salt
From your skin.

– SALT –

We were watching a T.V. show in the living room and it said, "Find a love that lasts a lifetime."
Mom was quick to interject, "Make a love that lasts a lifetime!"

I'm old enough now
To look past the
Breezy air
Of a fleeting romance
In summer

I'm longing for
The enduring warmth
That prevails
All winter long.

WINTER ROMANCE –

Then

When the firecrackers ceasefire
And the dancers have retired to their chairs

When the air is frigid and cold again
And the heat of gossip has passed

When the laughter's given way
To the hum of fluorescent lights

When the platters are void of food
And the eaters are empty of thoughts

When the nagging call of Monday
Becomes an imminent threat

When the euphoric drunkenness folds
Into a sappy and sober memory

When joy has lulled itself
Into a deep and boring sleep

Then

Do it then

Tell me
You love me.

– THEN –

Thank You

Mom, Sissy, Tre, Estella, Richard, Miguel, Rene, Yeshua, and everyone who supported my initial Kickstarter to publish this book. It's a dream come true.